In Our Neighborhood

Meet a Veterinarian!

by AnnMarie Anderson

Illustrations by Lisa Hunt

Children's Press®
An imprint of Scholastic Inc.

SCHOLASTIC

Special thanks to our content consultants:

Dr. Heather Wiedrick
Small animal veterinarian
Westernville, NY

Dr. Laurel Brenton
Small animal and exotics veterinarian
Monroe, NY

Library of Congress Cataloging-in-Publication Data
Names: Anderson, AnnMarie, author. | Hunt, Lisa, 1973– illustrator.
Title: In our neighborhood. Meet a veterinarian!/by AnnMarie Anderson; illustrations by Lisa Hunt.
Other titles: Meet a veterinarian
Description: First edition. | New York: Children's Press, an imprint of Scholastic Inc., 2021. | Series: In our
    neighborhood | Includes index. | Audience: Ages 5–7. | Audience: Grades K–1. | Summary: "This book
    introduces readers to the role of veterinarians in their community"— Provided by publisher.
Identifiers: LCCN 2021058729 (print) | LCCN 2021058730 (ebook) | ISBN 9781338768886 (library binding) |
    ISBN 9781338768930 (paperback) | ISBN 9781338768985 (ebook)
Subjects: LCSH: Veterinarians—Juvenile literature. | Veterinary medicine—Juvenile literature.
Classification: LCC SF756 .A525 2021 (print) | LCC SF756 (ebook) | DDC 636.089092—dc23
LC record available at https://lccn.loc.gov/2021058729
LC ebook record available at https://lccn.loc.gov/2021058730

10 9 8 7 6 5 4 3 2 1   22 23 24 25 26

Printed in Heshan, China 62
First edition, 2022

Series produced by Spooky Cheetah Press
Prototype design by Maria Bergós/Book & Look
Page design by Kathleen Petelinsek/The Design Lab

Photos ©: 7: Zoological Society of San Diego/Getty Images; 9: Ron Levine/
Getty Images; 13: Adam Williams/The Columbia Missourian/AP Images;
14: Iakov Filimonov/Dreamstime; 17: Juan Silva/Getty Images; 19 left: Olaf
Doering/Alamy Images; 19 right: Jessie Cohen/Smithsonian National Zoo/
Getty Images; 21: Peter Dench/Getty Images; 31 top left: Ivan Aleksandrov/
Dreamstime; 31 top right: Igor Terekhov/Dreamstime; 31 center: andresr/
Getty Images; 31 bottom left: Kcco08/Dreamstime.

All other photos © Shutterstock.

Table of Contents

OUR NEIGHBORHOOD

Hi! I'm Theo. This is my best friend, Emma. Welcome to our neighborhood!

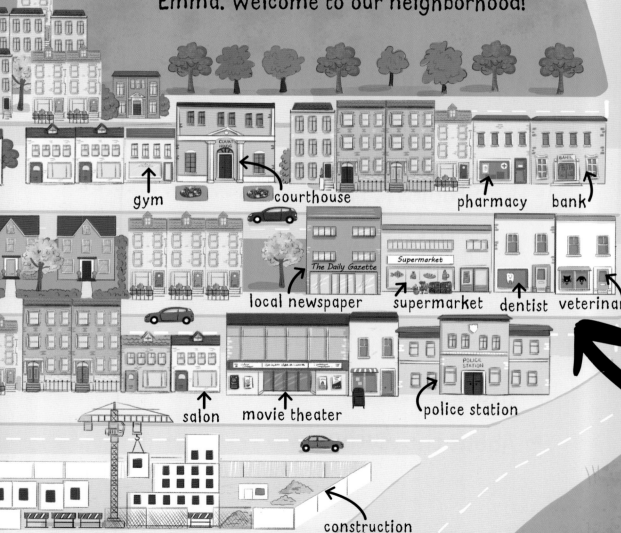

gym

courthouse

pharmacy

bank

local newspaper

supermarket

dentist

veterinar

salon

movie theater

police station

construction site

recycling center

fire station

hospital

restaurant

post office

library

school

café

The veterinary clinic is over there. Emma and I went there on Saturday while I was caring for our class pet, Freddy.

Freddy is our class bunny. It was finally my turn to take him home for the weekend. I was so excited!

I'm worried.

He doesn't want to play.

On Saturday, Emma came over to play with Freddy. But he wasn't acting like himself. My mom made an appointment to bring Freddy to the veterinary clinic.

Sunny will now what's wrong.

A veterinarian is a doctor for animals. Many vets work in clinics or animal hospitals. Some also work at national parks, zoos, and aquariums.

The clinic was busy. A vet tech named Amanda showed us to an exam room. She weighed Freddy and asked us about his diet.

Veterinary technicians, or vet techs, are like nurses. They help vets with different tasks. They draw blood, give first aid, take X-rays, and more.

What does your class feed Freddy?

Grass, hay, pellets, and vegetables.

MEET DR. SUNNY

When Amanda finished her exam, Dr. Sunny came in. Emma told Dr. Sunny that Freddy was scratching his ears and shaking his head a lot.

Dr. Sunny looked in Freddy's eyes and checked his teeth. Then he looked closely at Freddy's ears. Finally, he swabbed Freddy's ear.

Handling animals can be a messy job. Many vets wear scrubs, which are loose, comfortable, and easy to clean. Other vets wear a white lab coat over their clothes.

Dr. Sunny brought the sample to Amanda in the lab.
He let us come, too!

What's up?

Amanda looked at the sample under the microscope and told us what she saw.

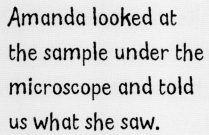

Freddy has ear mites.

It takes four years to complete veterinary school. Students learn mainly about dogs, cats, cows, and horses. Veterinarians who want to treat other animals usually get more training.

Dr. Sunny explained that ear mites are common in rabbits. Freddy would need medicine every two weeks for the next six weeks. We also had to replace Freddy's bedding and wooden chew toys.

I'll call your teacher to explain everything.

Please take a leaflet

Sometimes animals need surgery, just like people. A vet might have to pull teeth or remove an item a pet has swallowed by mistake.

Dr. Sunny showed us how to put the liquid medicine on the back of Freddy's neck. Then he put Freddy back in his crate and we got ready to leave.

ALL KINDS OF VETS

On Monday I brought Freddy back to school. Our classmates had a lot of questions about our visit to the vet.

What animals did you see there?

Some people don't live near a vet clinic. Pet owners might bring their cats and dogs to a mobile clinic for treatment.

Was Freddy scared?

We told our friends what Dr. Sunny had explained to us. Different types of vets work with different types of animals.

Small animal vets care for dogs and cats. They may also care for "pocket pets," such as rats, gerbils, hamsters, and rabbits.

Large animal vets are trained to treat livestock. That includes farm animals such as cattle, horses, sheep, goats, and pigs.

Exotic animal vets work with less common pets. Exotic pets include snakes, lizards, other reptiles, and birds.

Zoo and wildlife vets care for animals that live in zoos, national parks, and aquariums. That includes elephants, tigers, bears, and birds of prey.

The next day, our teacher, Mr. Garcia, had a big treat for the class. His sister is a vet who works with horses. Her name is Dr. Ember. We were taking a field trip to visit her at a horse farm!

I love horses!

Me too! This will be great.

Large animal vets often make house calls. They spend a lot of time on the road, traveling to ranches and farms to see their patients.

AT THE STABLES

Dr. Ember told us she visits the farm to give the horses regular checkups and to give them vaccines. Sometimes horses get injuries that need care.

Vets give animals vaccines. A vaccine is a shot that protects the animal from getting sick.

Today Dr. Ember was at the stables to do a checkup—on a baby horse!

This little guy is doing well.

We watched as Dr. Ember listened to the foal's heart and lungs. She made sure the baby was drinking its mother's milk. Then she checked to be sure its legs were straight.

He's so cute!

Vets use some of the same tools doctors do, like a stethoscope. The vet uses a stethoscope to listen to an animal's heart and lungs.

We had a great time at the farm! We learned all about what it's like to be a large animal vet. When we got back to school, we checked on Freddy. He was starting to feel better already!

Ask a Veterinarian

Emma asked Dr. Sunny some questions about his job as a vet.

How many years did you train to become a veterinarian?

Eight years. I went to college for four years. Then I studied in veterinary school for another four years.

Why did you become a vet?

I love animals, and I wanted to help keep pets healthy. When animals get sick, I like figuring out why and helping them feel better!

What is the most unusual animal you have ever treated?

I once treated a baby zebra.

What is the best thing about your job?

I love seeing the connection that develops between animals and their humans over the years.

What is one thing most people don't know about being a veterinarian?

It's important to have good communication skills when you are a veterinarian. Vets don't just care for animals—they work with their humans, too!

Dr. Sunny's Tips for Being a Responsible Pet Owner

- Take your pet to the vet regularly.

- Be sure your pet's vaccines are up to date.

- Make sure your pet gets plenty of exercise.

- Give your pet healthy foods and fresh water.

- Always clean up after your pet.

- Pets need love and attention, so play with your pet often!

A Veterinarian's Tools

Nail trimmer: Veterinarians use nail trimmers to keep a pet's nails at the proper length.

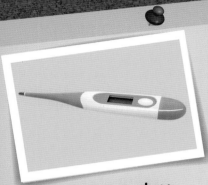

Digital thermometer: Veterinarians use a digital thermometer to measure an animal's temperature.

Scale: Veterinarians use a scale to weigh their patients.

Otoscope: Veterinarians use this tool to look inside an animal's ears and nose.

Ophthalmoscope: Veterinarians use this tool to look inside a patient's eyes.

Index

About the Author

AnnMarie Anderson has written numerous books for young readers—from easy readers to novels. She lives in Brooklyn, New York, with her husband, two sons, and her pet cat, Norman.